Me and my Dog

Maureen Galvani

Blackie
London

Bedrick/Blackie
New York

One day Daddy brought home a puppy.

Jodie Colletts

Copyright © 1989 Maureen Galvani
First published 1989 by Blackie and Son Ltd.

First American edition published in 1989 by
Peter Bedrick Books
2112 Broadway, Rm. #318
New York   NY   10023

British Library Cataloguing in Publication Data

Galvani, Maureen
Me and my dog.
I. Pets : Dogs – For children
I. Title
636.7

ISBN 0 216 92328 1

Blackie and Son Ltd.
7 Leicester Place
London WC2H 7BP

Library of Congress Cataloging-in-Publication Data

Galvani, Maureen.
Me and my dog/ Maureen Galvani –
1st American ed.
p.   cm.
Summary: A little girl describes the
antics of her pet dog Scruff.
(1. Dogs – Fiction. 2. Pets – Fiction.)
I. Title.
PZ7.G1422Me   1989
[E] – dc19   88-37368

ISBN 0-87226-409-2

Printed in Hong Kong

He looked so scruffy he made me laugh.

Every morning Scruff jumps on my bed and wakes me up.

He doesn't care if I'm still sleepy.

In the park I throw sticks for Scruff to fetch,

but sometimes he forgets to bring them back.

Scruff and I like playing outside...

but Mum makes us clean up our mess.

We often take Scruff out for a walk,

but he won't always go where we want him to.

Scruff looks forward to his dinner...

he'd really like to eat mine too.

Decorating is very hard work...

Daddy will be pleased that we are helping him.

I invite Scruff to my tea parties,

but he has very bad manners.

At Christmas
I give Scruff
a present.

It's just what he always wanted.

Scruff looks sad when I go off to playschool,

but he's always happy when I come home.

Scruff doesn't like having a bath,

but he enjoys giving us a shower.

Scruff helps me pack our favourite things...

when we go on holiday.